Rascal

LOST IN THE CAVES

CHRIS COOPER

ILLUSTRATED BY JAMES DE LA RUE

EGMONT

EGMONT
We bring stories to life

First published in Great Britain in 2015
by Egmont UK Limited
The Yellow Building, 1 Nicholas Road, London W11 4AN

Text copyright © 2002 Chris Cooper
Illustration copyright © 2015 James de la Rue
The moral rights of the author have been asserted

ISBN: 9781405275118

58624/1

www.egmont.co.uk

A CIP catalogue record for this title is available from the British Library

Typeset by Avon DataSet Ltd, Bidford on Avon, Warwickshire
Printed and bound in Great Britain by CPI Group

MIX
Paper
FSC FSC® C018306

Rascal

LOST iN THE CAVES

Collect all of Rascal's adventures:

For Megan Louise

CHAPTER 1

It all started with the big dog's bone.

Rascal could smell it before he saw it,
of course. The smell was coming from
the other side of a line of trees. He froze
for a second, sniffing the air. As usual,
there were new smells all over this place,

but that bone was the best of all.
Rascal followed his nose, making his
way through the cluster of trees. His
master, Joel, was somewhere back along
the path. He wouldn't mind if Rascal
did a little exploring for a minute
or two!

Rascal cleared the trees and there it
was on the grass – a nice big bone, the
kind with the marrow in the middle. It
was resting under one heavy paw of a

sleeping dog. A *big* sleeping dog.

Rascal padded forwards. The big dog was snoozing outside a wooden holiday cabin. It was small, just like the one Rascal was staying in with Joel and his family. He could hear people's voices from inside the cabin, but nobody came out.

Rascal wagged his tail in eager excitement. He forced himself not to run too fast. That would spoil the fun!

When he was close enough, he dropped to his belly and slid forwards. The sleeping dog let out a tiny noise – half grunt, half bark – that seemed to die in the back of its throat. It was probably dreaming about chasing cats.

Rascal inched on. He carefully placed his jaws around the tip of the bone and pulled. As the bone slid out, the big dog's paw flopped to the ground.

The dog's eyes opened. It was wide awake in an instant. It fixed the smaller dog with furious brown eyes.

Rascal's tail was wagging wildly. The bone dangled from his mouth. He was ready to play! A tug-of-war, a pretend fight . . . he was ready for anything. He let out a happy bark.

But the big dog's reply was very different. A deep growl escaped from its jaws. The growl built and built until it exploded into a fearsome bark. Then the big dog sprang to its feet. It glared down at Rascal menancingly.

Rascal was confused. He wasn't really stealing the bone! He was just having a bit of fun. But the big dog didn't see it that way. Not one bit, because suddenly it was lunging forwards and there was only one thing Rascal could do. Get out of there fast!

He whirled around and charged back the way he had come. He wasn't even aware that the bone was still clamped between his teeth. He didn't look back, but the big dog's angry pant told him all he needed to know. He was being chased.

Rascal burst through the trees, back to the footpath. His master was there now. Joel gave him a puzzled look.

'Rascal? What's wrong?'

Rascal raced up to Joel and huddled behind his legs.

'What have you got there?' asked the boy. He reached out a hand and took hold of the bone.

Rascal let out a nervous whimper. Joel's brow was creased in confusion. And then the bigger dog crashed through the bushes and on to the path. When it saw that Rascal had stopped, it slowed. It let out a low snarl as it came closer. Its ears stood on end and its tail slashed the air angrily. It was ready for a fight.

Rascal tried to disappear behind his master's legs. Joel stepped between the two dogs. His voice was calm as he spoke, but Rascal knew his master too well. He could hear the anxiety that bubbled under Joel's voice like a hidden stream.

'It's OK, doggie,' said Joel to the big dog. He lifted his arm slowly. 'This is yours, isn't it?' He was holding the bone out.

The big dog was watching suspiciously, as if this was some new kind of sneaky trick.

Joel let the bone fall to the ground.

'There you are,' he said. 'All yours.'

But the big dog didn't seem satisfied. It glared at Rascal and took another step forwards. Its growl became louder. Rascal pressed himself even closer to his master.

Joel didn't budge. 'No!' he said firmly

to the big dog. He didn't shout, but his voice was strong.

The dog paused, uncertain.

'Take the bone and go home,' Joel continued. He flicked the bone closer to the dog with one foot. 'Go on, now.'

The big dog took one last look at Rascal and Joel. Then it swept up the bone, turned and ran back the way it had come. The boy and his dog watched it go.

Joel began to wipe the flat of his hand against his jeans. 'Yuck! Dog spit!' He turned to Rascal. 'What were you up to anyway?' he asked.

Joel attempted to give Rascal a stern look, but the dog knew better than that. He jumped up and tried to give the boy's face a good licking.

'Get off, you crazy dog!' said Joel, but he was laughing and that just made Rascal try even harder.

Joel gave the dog a friendly shove, but Rascal was quickly up on his hind legs again. He was just too happy! He loved this place they were staying in.

Trees everywhere! No trim front lawns with flower beds that you weren't allowed to dig up! No having to wear a lead and no stopping at the kerb to look out for cars on the way to the park! Here he was free just to run and explore wherever he liked. It was great!

But more than all of that, he loved being here with Joel. That was the really good thing – spending all day, every day, with his master and best friend in the whole world. Every morning Joel was there and ready to play with him. *And* Joel was always ready to stand up for him, just as he had done with the big dog and its precious bone.

'Right!' Joel grinned. 'No more Mr Nice Guy!'

Rascal recognised those words. They were the signal for his favourite game – chase! He charged away, barking at the top of his voice. He didn't run too fast though, being careful not to get too far ahead of the boy who was pelting after him.

They had reached the bottom of the hill now. Rascal veered left off the path and doubled back through a clump of bushes. He could hear Joel behind him, the boy was right there, and then –

Rascal stopped.

Right ahead of him, sunk into the side of the hill, was a cave.

CHAPTER 2

The entrance to the cave gaped in the yellowish rock like an open mouth.

Joel had caught up with Rascal now. Like the dog, he too forgot instantly about the game of chase. 'Wow, look at that!' he said in amazement, and immediately began to cross the scrubby ground to get a closer look.

Rascal followed nervously. Something about the darkness of the cave made him uneasy. He stayed a short way behind Joel, who had reached the cave now. The boy took a couple of steps inside. The entrance was tall enough for him to stand, but the roof became lower almost immediately. Another few steps and his head would be bumping against rock unless he bent over. But then, *another* few steps and the daylight wouldn't have much effect on the cave's gloomy darkness.

'Can't see how far back it goes,' declared Joel.

Rascal peered into the blackness. He couldn't see much either, but that wasn't what was bothering him. There was the scent of something in there, something other than the cool dampness of the rock. The fur on the back of his neck rose.

It had to be an animal of some kind. But what was it? It wasn't rabbit and it wasn't squirrel, he knew those scents too well.

Suddenly something moved in the darkness ahead. It was as if a ragged patch of the blackness had ripped itself free and was tumbling towards him. A terrible, shrill scream tore through the air.

Rascal couldn't help himself. With a yelp of terror, he turned and fled.

'So what was it?' asked Joel's older sister, Catherine.

'A bat!' answered Joel. 'Well, there might have been more than one. It was hard to tell.'

Rascal was lying underneath the small table in the kitchen. They were back in the cabin. The family had eaten and now they were just sitting and talking. Usually, this was Rascal's favourite spot in the cabin. It was nice and warm and he could drift off to sleep to the sound of the family's voices. But tonight was different. He couldn't get comfortable, couldn't relax.

'Well, I hope you didn't take it upon yourself to go exploring,' said Joel's mum. 'Caves are dangerous places, you know.'

'Yeah,' said Catherine, grinning. 'You could get lost in there for ever. And years from now, kids round here would all tell the story of the haunted caves where you can hear the ghostly voice –' Catherine put on a pitiful whine here, the voice of a lost soul – '*Help me, my name is Joooooo-eeeeel.*'

Rascal's ears pricked when he heard his master's name, but he didn't get up.

'Hilarious, Catherine,' said Joel without a trace of a laugh. 'Hold on a moment while I roll around on the floor clutching my ribs.'

'It's true, though,' said Joel's dad from the other side of the room. 'You don't want to go poking around in caves.'

As he spoke, he had one knee on a
suitcase. He was struggling to zip it up.

'I know, Dad,' said Joel in a singsong
voice. 'We didn't stick around anyway.
You should have seen how fast Rascal
ran when that bat flew out!'

'Awww!' said Catherine.

The family laughed.

'Well, he's a city dog, isn't he?' said Joel's mum. 'He isn't used to the great outdoors.'

'You can say that again. Rascal probably thinks that food only ever comes out of a can!' added Catherine.

Joel ducked his head under the table. 'Are they making fun of you?' he asked. Rascal leaned forwards and sniffed at Joel's hand. It was empty. 'You're just a puppy, aren't you? It's not your fault if you got scared.'

'Well, he *acts* like a puppy, but I

wouldn't say he's exactly a puppy any more,' said Joel's mum.

It was true. Rascal was a young dog, but he was fully grown. He had thick black fur with a white patch on the chest. Whenever he was interested in something, his ears would prick up. As most things interested him, this often gave the dog a look of puppyish curiosity.

'We'd better not forget this tomorrow!' said Joel's dad. He was walking backwards and dragging something large into the room.

When Rascal saw what it was, his

heart began thudding. It was a travel
kennel, with one side covered in wire
mesh. A wave of unpleasant memories
flooded back to Rascal. How long ago
had it been? Two weeks?
Three weeks?

The family had driven to the airport. That's where Rascal had had to get into the travel kennel. Joel had put the dog's favourite chew toy in there with him. Then he had given the dog a solemn look and said, 'Don't worry, Rascal. It'll be OK.'

But it hadn't been OK, because then the kennel had been carried away! Panic had flared in the dog's heart. What was going on? The kennel had finally been put down in a noisy place where the view through the mesh was of nothing but stacks and stacks of cases.

It wasn't uncomfortable in there.

It was just confusing. And there had been the constant thought that he couldn't get out, even if he wanted to. Most of all, Rascal remembered the fear of not knowing when this would end. Now that same feeling of panic clutched at his heart.

Of course, Joel could tell Rascal was anxious. 'It's all right, boy,' he said gently, kneeling down to stroke his friend. 'We've got to go home tomorrow, and this is the only way dogs are allowed on to planes.'

''Fraid so,' said Joel's dad. 'And believe me, it'd be even worse if we had to drive the whole way back. It'd take us days.'

Joel's dad opened the mesh door of the travel kennel. The clang as it hit the side startled Rascal. It was too much for him. He yelped and ran for the door.

'Rascal!' cried Joel.

'There he goes again,' commented Catherine, and by then Rascal was already through the door and out into the cool of the evening.

The sky had faded to purple, but it was still warm outside. Rascal could hear no traffic noises, no distant wails of sirens. Instead, he was met by the relentless din of the crickets.

He didn't go far. He made it to the first line of trees that surrounded the cabin and stopped, hiding himself in the dark shadows.

A few seconds later the cabin door opened and Joel stood there.

'Rascal!' he called. 'Rascal!'

The dog looked at his master for a moment.

Joel called again. 'Come on, boy!'

Rascal couldn't wait any longer. He bounded up to his master. The two play-wrestled for a minute.

That was one of the great things about Joel. Even if you'd done something silly or run away or whatever, Joel wasn't the kind of boy who would make you feel bad about it.

'You're not the bravest dog in the world,' said Joel. 'But you're still *my* dog.'

He ruffled Rascal behind his ear in that spot he alone could hit just right.

He spoke quietly now. 'It won't be so bad, Rascal, I promise. Just a few hours in the kennel, that's all. And then we'll be home.'

Of course, Rascal didn't understand what Joel was saying, but as usual the boy's voice soothed him. Nothing could go wrong with Joel to look out for him, could it?

Joel stood now and patted his leg. 'Come on, boy,' he said. 'Let's go for a walk.'

The word 'walk' had the usual magic effect on Rascal. He sprang up eagerly and let out a little woof of excitement.

Joel headed off up the path. The hills were dark shapes all around them. They seemed to be shrugging their mighty shoulders in the breeze.

'Come on,' said Joel. 'This way.'

Rascal stuck with him this time. Once they got to the top of the hill, Joel sat down. Rascal flopped on to the grass next to him, resting his head against the boy's side.

It was quieter up here. As the sky darkened, the hills became less and less visible. The growing blackness seemed to wrap itself around him. Rascal had spent all of his life near the city, so he was used to the orange glow of streetlights at night. This was entirely different – the only lights visible came from the few other cabins that dotted the area. They seemed small and unimpressive compared to the swirl of sharp, bright stars in the sky above them.

Joel rested an arm on Rascal. They were quiet together for a long while, then Joel began to point out patterns of stars in the sky. To Rascal the boy's words were no more than a string of names without meaning, but that didn't matter. The dog looked up too.

Over to the east the wind was blowing a bank of dark clouds towards them. Rain was coming. Tomorrow they wouldn't be able to see the stars.

That was tomorrow. For now, Rascal just sat and listened and looked up at the night sky with Joel. The boy was pointing out one especially bright star that hung low in the sky. It was the same star that he always pointed out when the two of them were in the back garden at home. Somehow there was something nice about that thought. However far they might be from home, the same stars were looking down on them.

CHAPTER 3

Even before Rascal opened his eyes the
next morning, he knew the rain had
come. He must have heard it in his sleep.
It seemed as if all night his dreams had
been soggy with rain.

The bad weather only made him feel

even more uneasy now that the last day
of the holiday was here. Everything was
changing. The good weather had gone
and the family had packed their bags
– they were all stacked up next to the
cabin's front door. It was time to leave.

He heard muffled footsteps
from one of the bedrooms.
A member of the
family was up.
It was Joel!
Rascal's tail
began to thump
against
the floor.

When the boy came into the room, Rascal scrambled up, but Joel already had one finger to his lips.

'Shh! Quiet, Rascal!' he whispered, pulling on a jacket.

Rascal was up now. He lapped some water from his bowl, while Joel put a torch into his backpack. He picked up Rascal's lead too.

Rascal eyed it suspiciously, but relaxed when Joel shoved it into his pocket.

'We'll be back before the rest of the family's even up,' said Joel with a wink. He went to the front door. 'Come on, Rascal.'

The dog followed happily. There was nothing he liked better than walks with Joel!

Outside, the rain was falling heavily. Joel pulled up his collar. As for Rascal, a little rain wasn't a problem. He made a point of sloshing through the muddy puddles.

'Looks like you'll need a bath before we head home,' said Joel, grinning.

Rascal trotted alongside his master. Every so often he stopped and shook himself. Water sprayed out in all directions.

'Hey! Cut that out!' cried Joel.

They carried on down the path. It was a few minutes before Rascal realised where they were going. They were at the point where the path passed by the other cabin, the one with the big dog.

Joel pushed his way through a barrier of bushes and they were staring once again at the entrance to the cave. It didn't look any more inviting, even though it offered some protection against the rain.

'Come on,' said Joel. 'We'll just have a peek inside.'

Rascal held back a moment longer. Anxiety shifted inside him, but he forced it down. He wouldn't run away this time. He followed Joel to the entrance of the cave.

Inside, the rock beneath their feet was slick with water. 'Careful,' said Joel. 'It's slippy in here.'

He had taken the torch from his backpack and he clicked it on. A triangle of light sliced into the darkness of the cave. Water dripped down the walls. The cave was only a few metres wide, but it seemed to go back a long way.

Joel was edging forwards, steadying himself with one hand against the rock. He stooped low so his head wouldn't bump against the roof. 'Just a little further,' he said.

Rascal followed nervously. He almost leapt out of his fur when a big drop of water plopped on to the top of his head.

'It's only water,' said Joel, laughing. 'Hey, look! The roof gets higher again here.'

Joel was able to stand to his full height once more. He shone the torch around the cave now. It was wider and the floor was less smooth. The torch-light ran over a jagged cluster of stalactites that hung from the roof. Water dripped from them steadily. Rascal could hear the drops echoing as they added to the puddles of water around the cave.

Fear pressed down on him like a weight he couldn't shift. He didn't like this place, but he didn't turn and run. He wasn't a little puppy afraid of every shadow. He wasn't, and he would show Joel that he wasn't.

That's when Rascal caught the scent again, the same one he had smelled the day before. It had to be the bat! Well, he would show *it* who was afraid! He nosed ahead of Joel, growling in the back of his throat.

'Hold on, boy,' warned Joel from behind him. 'Let's not go too far in.'

But Rascal's eyes were growing accustomed to the darkness now. He picked his way through the wet rocks that made up the floor of the cave. Joel followed, trying to shine the torch's beam far enough ahead for the dog to see, but close enough that he could see where he was putting his own feet.

'Slow down, Rascal!'

Usually the dog would have listened – he *always* listened to Joel – but the smell of the bat was driving him crazy. It had to be close. Somewhere over his head maybe?

Suddenly something moved in the darkness. Rascal didn't see it as much as sense it, a ragged flapping in the

blackness. And then that awful screech!
It was the bat.

Rascal jumped up and let out a bark.
The bat flitted away, but when Rascal
landed, his front legs immediately
slipped forwards on the wet rock. Where
had the floor gone?

'Rascal!'

The torch-light behind Rascal
wobbled as Joel ran forwards to reach
out for him. The boy's hand closed
around one of the dog's legs, but Joel
couldn't save him. Instead they were
both falling, as if a hole had opened up
beneath their feet.

Rascal twisted in mid-air. There was a dreadful thud and a splash as they hit rock and water. The impact smacked Rascal's breath out of him and pain stabbed through his side and his back legs. It seemed as if star-bursts of light were exploding behind his eyes. Slowly they faded and all that was left was the darkness of the shaft they had fallen into.

A bitter smell mingled with the cave's musty one. There was no mistaking that scent. It was blood.

Joel!

CHAPTER 4

The boy was lying on his side, his face
turned downwards. The torch was
still on, but it was trapped underneath
his body so Rascal could hardly see
anything.

He sniffed at Joel. The boy was

unconscious, his breath coming in shallow pants. Rascal pressed closer. Joel had to wake up, he had to! Rascal licked at the boy's face, but the only response he got was a low moan.

Fear squeezed at the dog. It was his fault! He was the one who'd chased the bat. Joel had tried to save him and now Joel was lying here hurt.

What could he do? He turned round frantically, his paws sloshing in the water at the bottom of the narrow shaft. If he could just climb out of here, he could go and get help . . .

Rascal jumped up so that his front paws leaned against the rock face. It was slippery and went almost straight up. There was no way he could climb out. He tried a different spot. It was the same there too. There was no way he would be able to climb out of here.

Rascal flopped back down into the cold water at the bottom of the shaft. What now?

Maybe if someone heard him? If someone could bring help?

Rascal threw his head back and barked. He barked again and again until his barks ran together and he found himself howling into the black. The noise cut through the sounds of dripping water and echoed around the darkness.

When he stopped, there was nothing but the same old sound of falling water in the cave. It seemed to be mocking him.

Joel would know what to do, but Joel still wasn't stirring. Rascal bent his head to check the boy. And that's when he realised the terrible truth. The water at the bottom of the shaft was rising. At first it had lapped at his feet. Now it was part-way up his legs.

Joel! The boy's face was turned to the side, not far above the rock. If the water continued to rise, it would soon be covering his mouth and nose. Rascal burrowed his nose under Joel's shoulder and tried to turn him. He couldn't do it.

Rascal didn't give up. He took hold of the boy's jacket with his teeth and pulled. The material stretched taut. It looked as if it was going to rip. Rascal gave one last huge effort and pulled with all the strength in his body.

At last Joel flopped over on to his back. His face was clear of the water.

But the water was continuing to rise. Soon it would be as high as Joel's upturned mouth and nose. And then what?

There was only one thing for it. Rascal took the boy's hand between his teeth. It felt limp and cold. Gently, he pressed down with his teeth. He was careful not to bite hard enough to draw blood, but he had to bite hard enough for the boy to notice. Joel didn't wake up but he groaned and tried to pull his hand away.

It was difficult to do this to the person he loved most in the whole world, but Rascal forced himself. Once again he nipped at the fleshy part of Joel's hand, this time harder.

'Ow!'

Now Rascal let the hand go as it was snatched away. There was a moment's silence, but there was something different about this silence. It was the sound of someone trying to figure out what on earth was going on.

Rascal let out a bark.

'Rascal?'

The boy reached out. At first he was

just feeling for where the dog was, but
then he hugged his friend tight to him.
He buried his face in the side of the
dog's neck.

They stayed that way for a few
seconds, as if drawing strength from each
other.

Then Joel fished the torch out of the black water. Its beam was no longer very strong, but it still worked. He flashed the light up and down the sheer walls of the shaft. The beam stopped when it came to a break in the wall. About a metre up on one side, a small tunnel led off from the shaft. It looked narrow and dangerous.

Joel got to his feet slowly. When he put his weight on one ankle, he gasped with pain. He almost toppled over, but Rascal was there for him to right himself against.

'Let's have a look at this then.'

Joel bent and peered into the little tunnel.

'It's very narrow,' he said, and looked again at the sides of the shaft, trying to see if it was possible to climb out.

First he stuck the torch in a pocket in his jacket, then he ran his fingertips across the walls. He was looking for pockmarks or jutting rocks, anything that might help him climb up and out of here. There was nothing. The surface was smooth and made smoother still by the water that was pouring down it.

Joel looked at the water covering his feet. It was definitely higher now and it seemed to be rising faster. 'Where's it coming from?' he muttered anxiously. 'It can't all be the rain.' But Joel knew that it wasn't a matter of one hole filling slowly with rainwater. There were underground streams and rivers in many caves. Sometimes it didn't take all that much rain for them to overflow and flood surrounding tunnels and chambers. Sometimes it didn't take long at all for a chamber to go from a few centimetres of water to being completely flooded.

In one corner, a cluster of bubbles danced on the surface . . . which meant water had to be coming from somewhere under there.

What it came down to was this: they couldn't wait around for someone to discover they were missing, and then search the cave, and then find them here in this narrow pit. They would have to find their own way out.

Joel shone the torch again at the narrow tunnel in the side of the shaft. Its jagged shape looked like a rip in the rock. Would they even fit through there?

He didn't know, but one thing was certain: it was their only chance.

CHAPTER 5

Joel pulled himself into the tunnel first. The torch was too big for him to hold between his teeth, so he had to keep it in one hand. Its beam zigzagged as he crawled along on hands and knees.

If the tunnel had been wider, Joel

would have turned round to pull Rascal up. As it was, the boy's shoulders already bumped and scraped against the rock on either side. Joel waited just a little way inside the tunnel while Rascal tried to scramble up behind him.

It wasn't so easy for the dog. The first time, he fell back into the black water at the bottom of the pit. He launched himself at the tunnel entrance again, kicking his back legs frantically against the rock to push himself up.

Eventually it worked! He was right behind Joel.

The two began the slow crawl. It was hardest for the boy. Rascal wasn't able to stand fully but he could push himself along on his belly. After a while, though, the tunnel became too small for Joel to progress on hands and knees. He had to lie almost flat and wriggle along. It was easy to imagine all that rock above them. And what if the tunnel became even narrower? What if they got stuck?

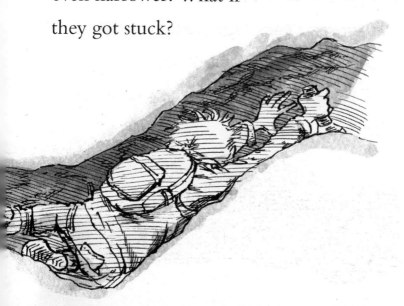

It was hard to chase away such terrible thoughts.

But at least the tunnel seemed to be going upwards, and their hopes rose with it. It was wet in here, but not as bad as the rising water in the shaft had been. They grew even more optimistic when the tunnel widened again.

But it wasn't all good news. The direction of the tunnel changed. It levelled off for a brief stretch and then it started to go gradually back downhill. As it did so, the water also began to get deeper and deeper.

Joel hesitated. 'I don't know about this,'

he said nervously. But he realised that there was nothing else for it. There was no chance of escape behind them. There probably wasn't even enough space for him to turn round here. All they could do was go on.

But the water was getting deeper and deeper. Rascal shivered as it lapped against his sides. He could hardly see beyond Joel to the light. He just knew that he had to keep following the boy.

Then Joel stopped.

'Oh no!' His voice was cracked with fear. He had reached a stretch where the roof of the tunnel suddenly dropped to the surface of the water. The tunnel continued, but it was full of water now.

The question was, for how long? Was this the end of the line?

Joel was leaning forwards, with his head turned back and one arm stretched into the tunnel ahead of him.

'I think it gets higher again,' he said, but the tremble in his voice betrayed his uncertainty. 'We've got to try it, Rascal.'

And with that, he took a deep breath, puffing his cheeks out. Then he ducked his head to clear the overhanging rock and pushed off into the tunnel.

Now that the torch-light had gone,

Rascal was in total darkness again.
His entire world was rock, water and
blackness. There was nothing for it. He
filled his lungs with air and pushed
forwards after his master.

Under the water was equally black,
but this was somehow different –
a *thicker* darkness,

one that seemed
to hide all hopes of escape.

His head scraped against rock above him. His chest throbbed and his heartbeat pounded in his ears. Any second now he would have to breathe out, then the water would come rushing in and that would be the end!

Suddenly one of his back legs slipped down. It had fallen into a crack. Rascal tugged, but it wouldn't come free. He started to panic.

A firm hand grabbed him in the blackness of the water. It took hold of his front leg and pulled him. Rascal let his back legs go limp. As they did, the one in the crack came free without difficulty.

And then Rascal's head burst out of the water. It hit the roof of the tunnel, but that didn't matter. All that did matter was that he could breathe again! He sucked the air in gratefully.

Joel pulled the dog clear. Rascal couldn't see it, but he could sense the boy smiling. However terrible things looked, there was always a chance as long as they were both still breathing.

Rascal was aware of something else now – a roaring sound, one that seemed quite close to them.

'You know what that is?' asked Joel. 'An underground river.'

CHAPTER 6

They made their way slowly through the rest of the tunnel without any more problems and finally they reached the tunnel's destination. The water poured down several metres into the rushing swirl of the underground river. To the right there was a narrow shelf of rock. Joel clambered out of the tunnel and on to this ledge. He helped Rascal do the same.

The boy shone the weak light of the torch on to the black water, which was flowing quickly. It was impossible to see how deep it was. Joel looked at its oily surface in desperation. What now?

But Rascal's mind was on other things. His nose had caught that bat smell once more. It came from somewhere above them. Bats had to have a way of going into and getting out of a cave, didn't they? That meant there must be a way out.

Rascal began to bark.

'What is it, boy?' asked Joel, but Rascal went on barking. Joel pointed the light towards the dog. When he saw that Rascal was peering upwards, he shone the light up the rock wall.

There was a wide crack high up in the wall. It looked just about big enough for them to get through, if only they could reach it. Joel raised one arm, but it didn't come close to the hole. He began to shine the torch on the narrow ledge as if he was looking for anything that might help.

'Come on,' he told himself. 'Think!' His voice was tight with panic now. Suddenly he knelt down next to the dog. His hands were at Rascal's neck. 'It's OK, boy. I'm just going to borrow your collar, that's all.'

He slipped the dog's leather collar off and, tucking the torch under his chin, pulled the dog lead from his pocket. He began working at it frantically. 'Hands are too cold,' he muttered, but at last he had the collar tied into a loop at the end of the lead.

He took hold of the other end and shone the torch-light on the rock that jutted out from the hole above them.

'Here we go,' he said, and he whirled

the collar and lead around a couple
of times to pick up speed and then
stretched up towards the rock with
them.

He came close,
but the loop
didn't fall
around the
rock.

Rascal watched in silence. Joel could do it, couldn't he? Joel *always* got him out of trouble.

But they had never been in trouble like this before.

'Try again,' said the boy, as if giving himself orders.

The second attempt was much like the first. Then, on the third go, the collar seemed to loop over the rock.

'Yes!' cried Joel, but almost immediately the collar came free when he tugged on the lead.

'It's no good. It won't work.' His words were weighed down with despair. He was giving up. Bitter tears rolled down his face.

This was more than Rascal could bear. He could sense the waves of fear and hopelessness coming from his master. It would be easy to give in, but Rascal wouldn't allow himself to be swept along by those feelings.

He began to sniff about the ledge. It didn't take him long to find the collar and lead. He picked them up with his teeth and turned to his master. He gave a little closed-mouth bark and pushed his nose towards Joel.

It was a few seconds before Joel spoke,

and then he said, 'One last try.' His voice sounded small and afraid in the darkness, but there was determination in it too.

Before he tried again, the boy turned to the dog. 'I'll never let anyone say that you aren't brave ever again, Rascal,' he said. Then, taking a deep breath, he swung the home-made lasso up.

Again the loop fell around the rock, but this time it stayed there. And it held fast when Joel tugged hard on the end that dangled free.

'We did it!' the boy cried. He bent to gave Rascal a great big hug, pressing his face into the fur of the dog's neck.

In the days and
months that followed,
the memory of that hug
would come back often to
Rascal.

Now Joel took hold again of the
lead with both hands. He leaned back
and began to walk his feet up the wall.
Slowly he hauled himself up, grunting
with the effort.

When he was near the edge, he let go
of the lead with one hand and threw it
over the rock. He wasn't able to grab on
to anything and he began to fall. His legs
kicked wildly.

Rascal was ready. The dog was
standing underneath his master and,
when Joel slipped, his foot landed on
Rascal's back. For a few seconds he bore
almost the complete weight of the boy.

The pain was terrible, but Rascal willed
his legs not to buckle.

At last Joel found a crack in the rock with his fingers. He gathered all his strength and pulled. His feet lifted clear of the dog's back. Now it was up to Joel.

Once the boy had pulled himself up enough, so that the top half of his body was lying flat, he swung one leg up to the edge of the rock. Rascal listened for a few seconds as Joel struggled and clambered over.

Then at last a voice spoke from the darkness above the dog. 'I did it, Rascal! *We* did it!' Joel flashed the torch-light around. 'It's a tunnel and it goes up. There's almost no water here.

I think it's a way out!'

Rascal let out a bark in reply. He could hear the excited relief in the boy's voice. But he could hear something else too – anxiety. They hadn't made their way to safety yet.

The next thing they had to do was to get Rascal up. Joel hung his head and shoulders back over the ledge. In one hand, he was holding the lead so that the leather collar hung down. In the other hand, he had the torch. He fixed Rascal in its spotlight.

'Here's what we're going to do,' he began. 'You've got to grab on to the collar. OK, boy? You just grab on to the collar and I'll do the rest.'

Joel jiggled the collar as if this was nothing more than an idle game, the sort of thing the two of them might get up to in the back garden on a lazy afternoon. The metal name-tag on the collar jingled softly against the sound of rushing water.

Now Joel was leaning over the edge as far as he could without toppling off. He stretched one arm down with the lead. The collar swayed just above Rascal's head.

The dog understood what he had to

do. He crouched down and then sprang
as high as he could. Pain flared in one
back leg, but he ignored it.
He snapped frantically at
the collar, but his teeth
closed on nothing
but air.

'That was great!' Joel said encouragingly. 'You just need to go a little bit higher, that's all.'

Rascal crouched once more. It felt as if he was gathering all his energy into a ball inside him. Then he released it, leaping as high as he could. And he reached the collar – his teeth actually brushed against it! But he wasn't able to get a strong enough grip.

He fell back again, but this time he didn't land on all fours. He had twisted too much as he jumped up and he fell back on his side.

'No!' screamed Joel.

Rascal hit the slope of rock and then the next thing he knew he was falling back again. Suddenly a thousand invisible knives were stabbing at his body. It was the icy water of the underground river.

Without thinking, Rascal thrust his snout up as high as he could. He sucked in a deep breath of air. He was kicking his legs frantically, but it was little use against a current this strong.

He heard Joel's terrified voice call out one last time: 'RASCAL!'

Then his head went under once again and there was nothing to do but let the current sweep him away.

★

Rascal had no idea how long he was carried by the black waters. Acting on instinct alone, he kept pushing his nose up to get air. And then he lifted his head once again, but this time it struck rock. The numbing pain was almost welcome as his mind fell back into a darkness every bit as black as the underground waters he was struggling in.

CHAPTER 7

When Rascal awoke, confusion clutched
at him. He was cold, freezing cold.
His eyes were open, but he could see
nothing.

Joel! Where was Joel?

A terrible image came back to him:

the look on his master's face as Rascal
had toppled back. And he heard again
the desperation and fear in the boy's
voice as he called out to the dog.

But where was Rascal now? The
tunnel was still filled with the sound
of rushing water, but he was no longer
being swept along. In fact, he was lying
in just a few centimetres of water. The
river must have carried him into a side
chamber where the current was much
weaker.

He got to his feet painfully and inched
forwards, not knowing if his nose would
strike rock at any moment. It didn't. He

padded on slowly, testing out the ground before him with one of his front paws. He kept the sound of the underground river to his rear.

Rascal began to realise that the water was getting shallower. After a few more steps, he became aware of something else too. It wasn't quite as dark now. He still couldn't see his own feet, but the pitch-blackness had grown lighter by a couple of degrees.

That's when he caught the scent. His nose told him that there had been humans around here. It wasn't Joel, but Rascal knew that any people might be able to help. Perhaps they were even in the cave to look for the missing boy and his dog?

Rascal let out a bark. There was no answer, but he wasn't discouraged. He didn't stop.

And then he saw it — a pale light in the distance up ahead. A way out! Rascal's heart began to do somersaults of happiness. He would see Joel again! He desperately wanted to run towards the light, but he forced himself not to. This was no time to have another accident.

Soon enough, he could see the sides and bottom of the cave. Now he could pick up speed a little, looking where to put his paws instead of feeling his way.

There were no people around now, but they must have been here quite recently, judging from the scent.

Finally he came to the entrance of the cave. It was still grey outside, but the light hurt his eyes after so long in total darkness. Rascal went on. This wasn't the entrance that he and Joel had gone into. It was much further down the hill.

He took one last look back into the cave and then stepped out into the open air. Rain was still pouring down and it was impossible to tell how long he had

been trapped in the caves. It had felt like
a very long time.

The dog was already soaking wet and the needles of rain felt good on his coat. They told him that he was alive and outside and free to find Joel again.

Rascal began to run up the hill. It was only now that he realised how tired he was. His body throbbed with pain. In particular, his back leg hurt from when he had fallen down the shaft. He could hardly put any weight on it. But that didn't matter. He could run on three legs for the moment. The important thing was to find Joel, to make sure that he was safe too.

A flash of lightning split the sky to his

left. The rumble of thunder followed almost immediately. That meant the storm was directly overhead. A memory suddenly came back to Rascal. When he had been a puppy, he'd been afraid of thunder. Joel had always gone to find him and brought him to his bedroom. Soon it had become a habit. Whenever there was a storm, the two of them would watch it through the window from the warmth and safety of Joel's room.

The memory of Joel made Rascal run even faster. It didn't matter how much it hurt. He was in familiar territory now.

He recognised the path here, knew the smells around him. It wouldn't be long until he reached the cabin.

He heard the sound of a car starting through the rain. An unknown fear gripped him and he plunged into the woods. He would take the short-cut to the cabin.

The car was moving now. Something about that noise sent him into complete panic. He ran faster, dodging between trees, leaping fallen branches and crashing through bushes.

He glimpsed a blur of red through the trees ahead. It was the car Joel's family had been using in this place. But where were they going?

More lightning flashed overhead. It seemed to be ripping the sky in half.

Rascal was running as fast as he could now. By the flash of the light, he saw who was in the car. Joel's mum was driving. Joel was in the back seat. His head was resting on his sister's shoulder and he was crying. Tears were rolling down his cheeks.

Rascal let out the biggest bark that he could, but, at exactly the same moment, the thunder boomed overhead. It was deafening and it drowned out all of his barks.

When the thunder ended, Rascal was still barking, but by now the car was a long way up the hill. He howled after it but was too far away to be heard.

Finally, as the car rounded the corner

at the top of the hill, Rascal just sat in
the rain and watched.

CHAPTER 8

Joel would come back for him, that's all there was to it. Rascal knew that Joel would never ever leave him. How could he? The two of them would always be together.

He took up position by the cabin,

knowing that the family would return. He didn't even care that he was cold and tired and wet. They would all come back and Joel would dry him off with a towel and give him his dinner. After that, Rascal would snuggle up in his favourite spot under the table and just drift off to the comforting sound of the family talking all around him.

But as the evening fell and the rain turned to a steady drizzle, no one came back to the cabin and doubts began to creep up on Rascal.

What if they didn't come back?

What if they had simply gone to the

airport to fly home for ever?

Suddenly he realised that Joel didn't think Rascal was ever coming back to the cabin. The boy had seen him fall back into the underground river, hadn't he? He'd watched as the dog's head disappeared under the jet-black water. Joel must have thought that he'd drowned!

That's why Joel was crying. He thought that Rascal was dead! That's why the family had left without waiting for him.

The dog slumped down in despair. He was all alone. The rain continued to fall. He was wet through to his bones, but he didn't care. He didn't care about anything.

Rascal felt suddenly more tired than he ever had before. It was like a great wave that rose above him and then crashed down, driving him once again into sleep.

But this was no restful sleep. Nightmares were never far away. In his troubled dreams, Rascal was completely alone in a dark, empty place where the wind howled and roared. The fear inside him was like a giant ball that grew and grew. The darkness seemed as if it was made entirely out of jagged rips of blackness that swirled around and around. But it wasn't this strange night that Rascal was afraid of. It was being alone, so very alone.

In the dream he could hear Joel shouting, 'Rascal! Come back! Please, come back!' but he couldn't see him anywhere. Rascal barked and barked, but he knew that Joel couldn't hear him over the noise of the wind. The black shapes swirled closer and closer until they folded around the dog and he fell at last into a deep and dreamless sleep.

He was shivering when he woke up. The rain had stopped now, but his coat was still waterlogged. The ground beneath him had turned to mud.

It was still dark, but he sensed that morning wasn't far away. The sun was waiting now for its time to rise. The smells of the woods were sharper than ever after the day's rainfall. Every bone in his body ached and a gnawing hunger filled his stomach.

Rascal lifted his head to the skies. He could see the stars through gaps in the clouds. They looked cold and distant at first. But as he looked up at them, he thought of Joel and how he loved to look at the stars.

Maybe right at this very moment, Joel was looking at the same stars. The thought filled Rascal with determination. If Joel couldn't come back for him, Rascal would have to make his own way back to Joel.

★

He forced himself to wait until the sun was up. He knew that he needed to gather strength.

Finally, when the grey light of early morning filled the forest, he rose slowly to his feet. That back leg still hurt when he put too much pressure on it, but he tried to ignore it. There were many miles to travel. He knew that he had to head for the direction in which the sun set. Now, with the morning sun behind him, he set off home.

He'd been going only a few minutes when he saw a man and a dog up ahead. They were out for an early-morning walk. As they approached each other, Rascal realised that he had met this dog before.

It was the one with the bone, the one that had chased him just two days ago.

The dog was off the lead. It was trotting on in front of its owner, and what's more it still had the bone clamped between its jaws.

Maybe it had stayed that way for the whole two days, just in case any other thief decided to try its luck!

The big dog's eyes narrowed as they fell on Rascal. Its tail wagged furiously. Rascal was too tired to do anything but keep on walking.

The dog's owner called to the big dog now. 'Come away, Samson.' He gave Rascal a dismissive look. The dog's fur was matted with mud and he had no collar around his neck. 'I don't want you going near a stray like that!' added the man. The big dog hesitated a moment and then trotted on..

Rascal just put his head down and continued on his way. That's what he was now, a stray, and that's how he would stay, for as long as it took, until he was reunited with Joel.

Suddenly he heard a scurry of paws behind him. It was the big dog again. Rascal turned, though he knew that he didn't have the energy to fight. But the big dog wasn't looking for a fight today. It walked up to Rascal and dropped the bone. It looked quite a bit more chewed than it had done, but still pretty delicious! The dog gave one short, deep bark, then bounded back to his owner.

Rascal bent his head and swept up the
bone in his jaws. He began to crunch
hungrily. For the next few minutes, he
didn't think of anything else. He was
careful not to let a single scrap of meat
or marrow from the bone go uneaten.

At last he was done. His stomach wasn't full, but the hunger wasn't so bad now.

And, as the morning sun warmed his back, he was more hopeful too. The journey would be long but he knew he would see Joel again. And all journeys must begin in the same way – Rascal fixed his eyes on the horizon and took his first step home.

Now Rascal has to find his way
home to his best friend Joel!
His next adventure begins in this
special extract from

TRAPPED ON THE TRACKS ...

CHAPTER 1

Steak! That's what Rascal had been thinking about when he saw the squirrel. A great big, fat, juicy steak . . .

It wasn't as if he'd always eaten like that in the old days, back when he still had a home. Just once, as a special treat, his owner, Joel, had given him steak for dinner.

'Don't go getting used to this,' Joel had laughed, and then he had ruffled Rascal's ears. The memory of that steak kept Rascal going now. He could smell it. He could even imagine the wonderful juices trickling down his chin as he bit into it.

There was just one problem. Here he was, out in the middle of nowhere. There was no Joel, there was no steak. Nothing but trees. It seemed as if he had been running through this forest all morning. He hadn't seen any other animals, but from time to time he'd been aware of unseen eyes watching him.

Once or twice he'd heard a rustle of leaves and caught sight of a pair of small back legs disappearing from view.

His hunger was like a ball of emptiness in his stomach. It just got bigger and bigger as the day slipped by. He sniffed at some berries on a bush. He'd seen the birds eating them, but he couldn't bring himself to taste one.

He'd have to get a bit more desperate before he started eating bird food!

That's when he spotted the squirrel. It was on the ground, holding an acorn in its paws and looking around primly. It didn't seem to have noticed him.

Rascal had never hunted an animal in his life, but now his hunting instincts kicked in. He charged forward. By the time the squirrel looked up, it was too late.

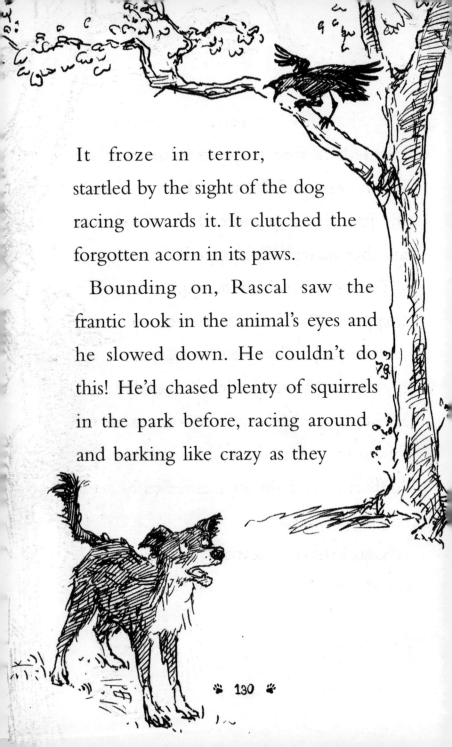

It froze in terror, startled by the sight of the dog racing towards it. It clutched the forgotten acorn in its paws.

Bounding on, Rascal saw the frantic look in the animal's eyes and he slowed down. He couldn't do this! He'd chased plenty of squirrels in the park before, racing around and barking like crazy as they scuttled up into the trees. But that had been very different — that was only for fun. Chasing squirrels for food was another matter. He stopped.

The squirrel seized the opportunity. It snapped out of its frozen state and pelted up a nearby tree. Once it was high enough, it chattered angrily at the dog. 'Tchhrrrr!' Its voice was joined by the harsh cry of a crow in another tree. It almost seemed to be laughing at Rascal.

Rascal barked, although his heart

wasn't really in it. The crow didn't budge, but the squirrel disappeared into the branches. Rascal would have to find something else to eat. But what?

He realised he was at the edge of the forest. He poked his nose out warily. It was good to see sky again. The sun wasn't far from its highest point. Rascal was glad to see it so that he could be sure he was still going in the right direction. Home. As long as he kept going west . . . he knew it with a certainty that came from deep inside him. If he was ever to see Joel again, he had to keep on going west.

He paused and looked at what lay beyond the trees. Not much really – at least not much to a dog like Rascal, who had grown up in the city. Train tracks hugged the edge of the forest, separating the trees from a patchwork of neat fields. The fields stretched in front of him and at the far end of them sat a large house.

Rascal's ears pricked up with interest.

A house meant people, and people meant food . . . maybe. OK, it was too much to expect a steak dinner there, but he might be able to beg some scraps. It was worth a try. The ache in his legs told him that he couldn't go much further without food.

He stepped carefully over the train tracks, making sure he didn't get a paw stuck in the deep grooves between the metal rails. Then he ran down the embankment.

It was easy getting into the field through the fence. Rascal just flattened himself and crawled on his belly under the lowest bar.

He began to trot through the first field.
It felt good to be in the open air again
and just the chance of a decent meal at
journey's end gave him more energy.
A herd of cows huddled on the far side
of the field. They were too interested in
eating grass to notice Rascal. Every so
often one of them let out a bored moo.

Rascal couldn't imagine living on a diet of grass – yuck! Grass was for rolling in, not eating, wasn't it?

He was halfway across the next field when it happened. At first Rascal thought that a bee had whizzed past his ear. But then there was a sharp CRACK!